The Best-Ever Adventure

Eric Artisan

The Best-Ever Adventure

Once upon a time . . .

. . . a young prince and princess lived very happily.

Their kingdom was the
most wonderful place . . .

. . . and they had everything
their hearts desired.

They were full of life . . .

. . . and wanted to experience as much as possible.

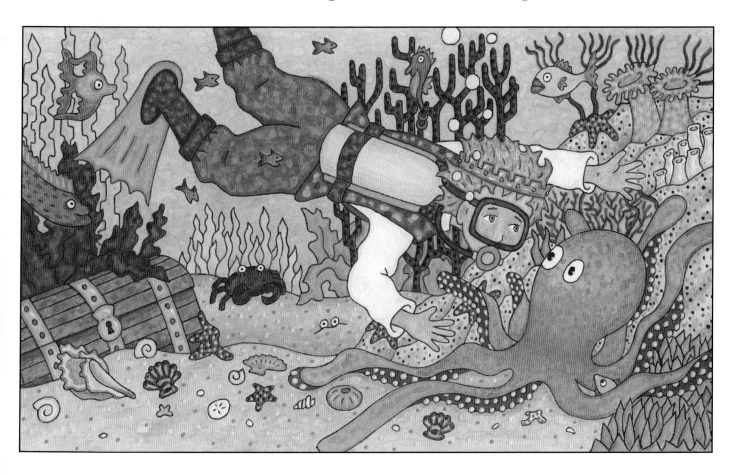

"Everything?" asked the wizard.
"Are you sure? Everything
is a *lot*, you know."

"Yes!" they replied.
"The more the better!"

"Well, 'everything' means the *bad*
as well as the *good*," said the wizard.
"Are you willing to experience *both*?"

"Well, 'bad' is difficulty. It is
a challenge to overcome. And
it is *not* something you can
experience here in the Kingdom."

"You must travel to another land,
where there are also many
wonderful things to experience
that wouldn't be possible
without the bad."

"Yay! A great adventure!
And a whole new land to explore!
How soon can we go?"

"Understand that to *truly*
experience this place, you must
live as everyone else lives,
and you cannot just pretend."

"When you go, you must *forget* you are the prince and princess, and you must leave all that you know behind."

"The only way to reach this land is
by crossing the Great Sea of Possibility. . . .

"Once you experience all that you set out to do, you can easily return."

And so they sailed away
from their peaceful kingdom . . .

. . . with a great sense of adventure.

Upon arrival, they instantly forgot
their royal heritage. . . .

They even forgot they were brother and sister, and they went their separate ways, alone.

Life here was much harder than in their kingdom,
and they both faced many difficulties.

There were so many choices to make!
And they didn't always make the right ones.

Never before had they suffered.
For the first time, they experienced
sadness, anger, fear, and pain.

Never before had they experienced
limitations. Here they could not
always have things their own way.

And never before did they have to think
and act creatively to overcome
obstacles and challenges.

Sometimes it could be lots of fun!

They experienced so many things that
did not exist back in their kingdom.

And in this new place they could experience
such a variety of thoughts and emotions.

Some of the best feelings came from
receiving kindness and help from strangers . . .

. . . as well as from helping others in need.

Feelings of love and friendship
were especially cherished.

And there were so many different
types of people to meet!

Although here they could feel fear . . .

. . . they could also feel courage.

Although here they could feel anger . . .

. . . they could also feel forgiveness.

Although here they could feel selfishness . . .

. . . they could also feel generosity.

Although here they could feel sadness . . .

. . . they could also feel hope and new joy.

Experiencing the "bad" . . .

. . . made experiencing the good so much better!

But most importantly, they *learned*
from their bad experiences.

The prince lived a long life, experiencing
many things. Then one day, like everyone
who visits this land, he passed away.

The princess, too, eventually came to
the end of her grand adventure.

But no sooner did their adventures end there
than they awoke at home in their kingdom.

Oh, they were so happy to
see each other again!

"Welcome back!" the wizard greeted them.
"Did you experience everything
you wanted to?"

"Oh my goodness!
That was so *hard!*"
said the princess.

"No kidding! I'll
never do that again!"
said the prince.

"Ah! But consider all that you
have learned," said the wizard.
"Do you think your experiences
have caused you to *grow* in any way?"

"Have they helped you become
a better person? More compassionate,
perhaps? More understanding?
Wiser in the ways of the Universe?"

"Well, yeah, I guess so,"
they both replied.

And so they told each other everything
they had experienced and learned
on their journey.

They talked about all the good things
they enjoyed, as well as the bad.

They remembered all the many things
unique to that world.

They considered how they could have
done things differently—better.

And they realized there was still
so much they had not yet experienced.

So, one day . . .

. . . long after their first adventure . . .

. . . knowing they would
always return home . . .

The
End

(The adventure
continues...)

Thanks, Mom. Once again, I couldn't do this without you.

And thank you, Laura, for your encouragement and support.
Your friendship means the world to me.

And much thanks to John Thompson and Breanna Powell at
Illumination Arts for their publishing and design assistance.

Most of all, thank *you*, my readers —
thanks for spreading the word.

Please consider donating copies of *The Best-Ever Adventure* to your
local schools, libraries, and children's hospitals.
Thank you.

EricArtisan.com

ISBN 978-0-578-61441-0

Published in the United States by Eric Artisan Books
Manufactured in China

Book design by Breanna Powell Design

Eric Artisan is a contemporary artist, writer,
and book lover. He's also author of the amazing
novels *Escaping the Wheel* and *Vengeant*.
Drop him a line at EricArtisan.com.

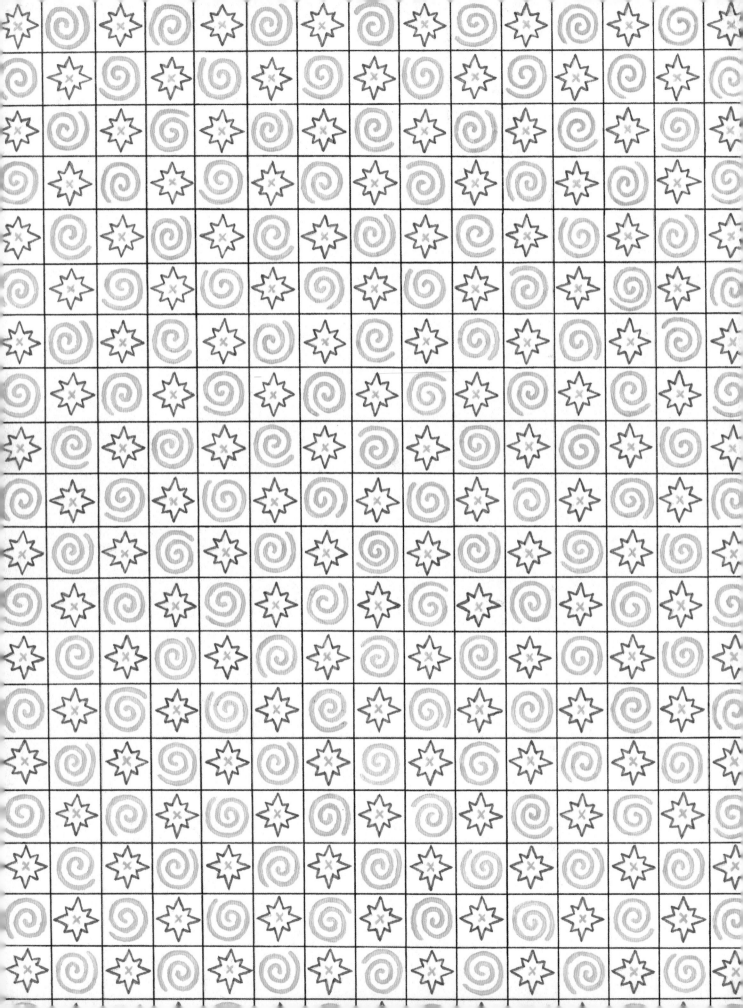